W9-CCF-746

Winter's Coming

A Story of Seasonal Change

Owl
kids

By Jan Thornhill

Illustrated by Josée Bisaillon

The leaves were just beginning to change color in Lily's forest home. Lily was a young snowshoe hare, not even six months old. She'd never seen anything other than green on the trees, so the new colors were a surprise.

Lily spent her days hopping from here to there, nibbling on leaves and tender twig tips and bark. Usually, she moved slowly, keeping her ears open for danger. If she kept still, she blended in with the colors of the forest floor and was difficult to see.

Sometimes, though, she couldn't help but leap into the air for the sheer fun of it. Lily had powerful back legs, so she was a good jumper.

One day, there was a crazy racket high in the treetops.
Lily glimpsed a few flashes of shiny black feathers through the
foliage. Then a wingtip. Then a beak. With a great rustling of leaves
and flapping of wings, a hundred birds descended to the ground.

Lily had never seen such a huge flock. "What's going on?" she asked.

"Winter's coming," said a grackle, "so we're flying south."

Lily looked around nervously. She knew about the danger of
coyotes and foxes and owls but had never heard of Winter. If the
birds were trying to escape from it, maybe she should, too.

She tried springing upward while flapping her arms as hard
and fast as she could, but—PLOMP!—down she came again.

"Silly," laughed a red-winged blackbird. "Snowshoe hares can't fly."

"They don't go south, either," said another.

With that, the flock took off and disappeared beyond the trees.

Lily was wondering if Winter could fly like a blackbird, when she spotted a red squirrel in a spruce tree. He was nimbly balancing a mushroom cap in the crook of a branch.

"Why are you doing that?" asked Lily.

"I'm drying this mushroom so I can store it with the others I've collected," said the squirrel. "I've got a big pile of spruce cones stashed away, too."

"Why do you need to hide so much food?"

"Because Winter's coming."

If Winter had such a big appetite that the squirrel had to hide his food from it, maybe Lily needed to worry about her own food.

"Should I be hiding what I eat, too?" she asked.

"No need," said the squirrel. "Even when Winter's here, hares can always find enough twigs and bark to keep their bellies full."

"Whew!" thought Lily. Whatever Winter was, at least it wasn't interested in her food.

Lily was wondering if Winter could leap from branch to branch like a squirrel, when she heard the soft call of a chickadee. The tiny bird was using his beak to wedge something into the bark of a tree.

"What are you doing?" asked Lily.

"I'm storing food before Winter gets here," said the chickadee. "I've got thousands of seeds hidden."

"Why don't you fly away like other birds do?" asked Lily. "Aren't you afraid of Winter?"

"Bah!" said the chickadee. "I've got lots of food, and, just like you, I know how to keep warm when it's cold out."

The chickadee was right about Lily knowing how to keep warm. Even though the nights were getting much colder, her thick fur always kept her cozy. But what did the cold have to do with Winter? Did Winter only come when it was cold?

Lily was wondering if Winter would have a soft call like a chickadee or a harsh one like a grackle, when a mosquito landed on her nose and poked her with its long proboscis.

"Yow!" cried Lily. "What'd you do that for?"

"Sorry, my dear," said the mosquito, "but I just need a wee drop of your blood so I can lay my eggs in the marsh. They'll be safe from Winter in the water beneath the ice."

"But what about you?" asked Lily. "What are you going to do when Winter comes?"

"Oh, me?" said the mosquito softly. "Well, Winter will kill me. But when it warms up again," she added brightly, "the ice will thaw and my eggs will hatch, so there will be lots of my babies to take my place!"

Lily's eyes widened with alarm. "Will Winter kill me, too?" she asked.

"Don't be ridiculous," said the mosquito. "Winter doesn't kill snowshoe hares!"

"Thank goodness," said Lily, but she felt sorry for the mosquito.

Lily was wondering if Winter would have a sharp-tipped
proboscis and long, dangly legs like a mosquito, when she came
upon a gray tree frog trying to slither under a rock.

"Why are you trying to squeeze under there?" she asked.

"Because Winter's coming," croaked the frog.

"So you're hiding?" asked Lily.

"Well, I don't call it 'hiding.' I call it 'hibernating.'"

Whatever fancy word the frog chose, it looked like hiding to Lily. And if the frog thought it was a good idea, maybe Lily should hide, too.

She tried to dig under a bigger rock with her forepaws, but she soon stopped. She wasn't a good digger and, besides, the rock was unpleasantly cold.

"Brrr." She shivered. Under a rock was not a good hiding place for a snowshoe hare.

Lily was wondering if Winter clung to branches with sticky toe pads like a tree frog, when she almost stepped on a woolly bear caterpillar. He seemed to be searching for something on the forest floor.

"Can I help?" asked Lily.

"Oh, no. I'm just looking for a safe place to curl up under these leaves."

"Because Winter's coming?" guessed Lily.

"Yup," said the caterpillar. "When I find the perfect spot, I'll curl up and freeze as solid as an acorn."

Lily was horrified. "That sounds awful!" she said.

"Oh, no—it's just like sleeping," said the caterpillar. "And when Winter's gone, I'll thaw out, eat some more, and then spin my cocoon."

"Maybe I could curl up under the leaves with you," said Lily.

"I wouldn't advise it," said the caterpillar. "Hares aren't made to freeze. Me, though, I'm special."

"But Winter's coming. What am I supposed to do?" asked Lily.

But by then the caterpillar had disappeared beneath the leaves.

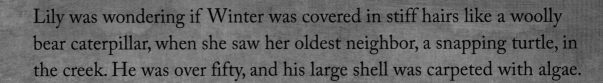

Lily was wondering if Winter was covered in stiff hairs like a woolly bear caterpillar, when she saw her oldest neighbor, a snapping turtle, in the creek. He was over fifty, and his large shell was carpeted with algae.

"See you next year!" he said.

"What do you mean 'next year'?" asked Lily.

"I'm going to bury myself in the mud at the bottom of the creek, where I'll stay until the weather warms up again."

"Are you doing that because Winter's coming?" Lily asked.

"You got it, kid," said the snapper.

"Could I hide in the mud under water with you?" asked Lily.

"Oh, no," said the snapper. "You're a hare. You'd drown."

"But how can you breathe under water?" asked Lily.

"We turtles have our ways," said the old snapper, "but they won't work for you."

With that, down he dove.

Winter was sounding more and more mysterious to Lily. She couldn't stop thinking about what it would look like. Would it have a hard shell and sharp beak like a snapping turtle? Or would it be completely unlike anything she had ever seen before?

Would it be as tall as the trees and have humongous, smelly feet? Or would it be stretched out like a weasel, with a hundred pointed teeth? Would it have a bald head like a turkey vulture? Or would it have hair so long that it swished along the ground? Would it make a noise like thunder? Or would it fly on silent wings like an owl? Lily had no idea, but she was convinced that Winter would be big and powerful.

More than a month and a half had passed since Lily had first heard about Winter. One day, she bumped into a black bear. He was filling a hole at the base of an uprooted tree with leaves.

"Why are you doing that?" she asked.

"I'm preparing a den for Winter."

Lily was about to ask the bear why Winter couldn't prepare its own den—was it simply too lazy?—when a strange white flake landed on her nose. She went cross-eyed trying to look at it…but it had already disappeared.

More white flakes fell from the sky. Some of them landed on the ground. A few caught in the bear's fur.

"Look!" said the bear. "Winter's here!"

"What?!" said Lily. "Where?!" She spun around, looking for Winter, but all she could see was the stillness of the leafless forest—and more of those strange white flakes falling from the sky. She peered closely at the leaves at her feet. Maybe she was wrong about Winter being big. Maybe Winter was incredibly tiny.

"I don't see anything," she said. "Where's Winter?"

The bear looked at her quizzically. "What do you mean? Can't you see the snow? It always snows in the wintertime."

"Winter is…a time?" Lily said quietly.

"Mm-hmm," said the bear. "Winter is a season. It's when it gets cold outside."

"Is summer a season, too?" asked Lily.

"Yup. And so is fall," said the bear. "Winter is when we get freezing temperatures and ice and snow. There won't be any insects or berries for me to eat, so I make a den where I can curl up and sleep until spring comes."

"Shouldn't I do something to prepare for Winter, too?" asked Lily.

"You already have," said the bear. "Look what's happened to your coat."

Lily had been so preoccupied with what Winter would look like, she hadn't noticed that her own fur was now almost completely white.

By the next morning, the forest was covered in a deep layer of snow. Lily was nearly invisible...

...even when she leaped into the air for the pure fun of it.

Animal and Environment Facts

Snowshoe Hare

The snowshoe hare got its name from its oversized back feet that, like snowshoes, are spread out enough to keep the animal from sinking in deep snow. This is helpful when a hare is being chased by a heavier, small-footed predator—a fox or coyote is more likely to get bogged down in snow while the hare can hop to safety. It can take more than a month for a snowshoe hare's fur to change color, once in fall and again in spring.

Grackle and Red-Winged Blackbird

Grackles and red-winged blackbirds are close cousins and can often be found nesting near one another in marshes. In their wintering grounds, they sometimes form flocks of several million birds, along with cowbirds and starlings. These "super flocks" roost together at night but break up during the day to search for food.

Red Squirrel

A single red squirrel can harvest more than 15,000 spruce cones in a single season. Because they depend on their stockpiles of food to make it through winter, they are very territorial. When a squirrel's home ground is invaded by another squirrel—or even a human—it instantly goes on the defensive by aggressively flicking its tail and chattering loudly.

Black-Capped Chickadee

Chickadees are so tiny they weigh less than two quarters. They have to eat as much as they can during the day because they burn off all of their stored body fat each night while they sleep. When it's very cold, they can lower their body temperature to make their food energy last longer. In the summer, along with seeds and berries, they eat enormous numbers of insects—so many they are considered an important forest-pest exterminator.

Mosquito

The mosquito's main source of energy is not blood but sugar, which it gets from plants. But a female needs a blood meal to produce her eggs. After being bitten by a mosquito, you might get an itchy welt—this is caused by a mild allergic reaction to the mosquito's saliva. There are around 150 different mosquito species in North America and 3,000 in the world.

Gray Tree Frog

The gray tree frog has mottled gray to green skin with egg-yolk yellow under its thighs. It can change color like a chameleon to match its surroundings—except during winter hibernation, when its color turns to blue! It has sticky pads on its feet that allow it to cling to almost any surface.

Woolly Bear Caterpillar

The woolly bear caterpillar is the brown-and-black banded larval stage of the Isabella tiger moth. Folklore suggests that the width of the middle band of these caterpillars can be used to predict whether or not the coming winter will be harsh. Though most scientists disagree, there is some evidence that if the previous winter was mild, the size of the middle band might be wider than usual.

Snapping Turtle

In the summer, snapping turtles prefer to lounge in shallow water with only their nostrils sticking above the surface. They choose winter hibernation spots where the water is deep enough that it won't freeze. Females don't lay their first eggs until they are 15 to 20 years old.

Black Bear

Black bears begin preparing for winter in late summer by gorging on foods such as berries and grubs to put on a thick layer of fat for the winter. When it gets cold out, the bear curls into a tight ball in its den and covers its head with its front paws. In January, a pregnant female black bear wakes just long enough to give birth, then goes right back to sleep. The cubs suckle and grow, while their mother continues her hibernation.

How Animals Prepare for Winter

Winter can be tough on animals. Temperatures often drop below freezing, and deep snow can make it difficult to move around. Food can be hard to come by or it can disappear entirely. Animals have developed all kinds of different ways to deal with these hardships.

Let's Get Out of Here!

Many bird species, and a few types of bats and insects, escape winter by migrating—they fly long distances to areas where they can stay warm and find enough food to eat. Traveling so far takes an enormous amount of energy, and many migrators do not complete the journey. Blackbirds, warblers, flycatchers, swallows, ducks, herons, and many other types of birds are migrators.

I Think I'll Just Go to Sleep

A number of animals that can't find food in the winter simply hide away somewhere. Mammals that sleep through the winter put on extra fat by eating a lot during the late summer and autumn. Black bears, chipmunks, and skunks go into torpor, a deep slumber where their breathing and heart rates slow down. During warm spells, these animals can wake up and sometimes even go for short walks.

True Hibernators

Other mammals, such as groundhogs and jumping mice, are true hibernators. Their body temperatures can fall to a few degrees above freezing, and their breathing and heart rates can slow so much they can seem almost lifeless.

Underwater Hibernation

Snapping turtles sleep away the winter buried in mud at the bottoms of creeks and ponds. When they're hibernating, snappers keep their open mouths above the mud and get just enough oxygen from the water to keep them alive. Some amphibians, such as the bullfrog and the red-spotted newt, survive winter under water by "breathing" through their skin.

Frog-Sicles and Cater-Sicles

A few frogs—such as the gray tree frog and the wood frog—actually freeze! As the weather gets colder, their bodies produce a type of sugar called glucose. Though ice forms in all the spaces around their cells, the glucose keeps the insides of their cells from freezing. Woolly bear caterpillars are also freeze-tolerant. Some can even survive Arctic winters!

Save the Children!

Even though many adult insects cannot survive freezing temperatures, their eggs, nymphs, larvae, or pupae can in different ways. Mosquito eggs are laid in water and survive unharmed beneath the ice. Praying mantis females provide an insulated case for their eggs. Some beetle grubs burrow below the frost line in soil—others are protected deep inside fallen logs or tree trunks. The aquatic nymphs of some insects, such as dragonflies, remain active under water throughout the winter. Still other insects survive the cold months as pupae—giant silkworm moths wait inside cozy cocoons wrapped in leaves.

Put on Your Snowsuit

Many species of mammals adapt to winter conditions by growing a thicker insulating layer of down and longer hair—the white-tailed deer grows hollow hair for extra insulation. Other mammals, such as the snowshoe hare and the weasel, trade their summer colors for snow-white camouflage. Smaller mammals, such as deer mice, don't grow a thicker coat of fur. Instead, they create networks of tunnels beneath the snow, which provides a cover as warm as a giant duvet.

Fluff Balls

When it's very cold, chickadees and other non-migratory birds fluff out their feathers and shiver to produce heat, which is then trapped in their undercoats of down. Their featherless legs are warmed by the special way their blood vessels are arranged—and they can always stand on one leg while tucking the other into their downy winter parkas!

Fill Your Pantry!

Many winter-active rodents, such as squirrels and deer mice, stock up on food before the ground is covered in snow. Red squirrels store dried mushrooms in tree nests and make huge stockpiles of pine and spruce cones. Gray squirrels bury nuts. Chickadees and nuthatches hide, or cache, seeds in the bark of trees. Amazingly, these animals all have excellent memories of where they have stashed their food.

To Isabelle and Marion. Seasons change, friendship stays — J.B.

Owlkids Books acknowledges the financial support of the Canada Council for the Arts, the Ontario Arts Council, the Government of Canada through the Canada Book Fund (CBF) and the Government of Ontario through the Ontario Media Development Corporation's Book Initiative for our publishing activities.

Published in Canada by
Owlkids Books Inc.
10 Lower Spadina Avenue
Toronto, ON M5V 2Z2

Published in the United States by
Owlkids Books Inc.
1700 Fourth Street
Berkeley, CA 94710

Library and Archives Canada Cataloguing in Publication

Thornhill, Jan, author
     Winter's coming : a story of seasonal change / by Jan Thornhill ; illustrated by Josée Bisaillon.

ISBN 978-1-77147-002-5 (bound)

     1. Animals--Wintering--Juvenile fiction. 2. Winter--Juvenile fiction.   3. Seasons--Juvenile fiction. I. Bisaillon, Josée, 1982-, illustrator II. Title.

PS8589.H5497W56 2014   jC813'.54   C2014-900387-0

Library of Congress Control Number: 2014931866

Edited by: John Crossingham and Karen Li
Designed by: Barb Kelly

Manufactured in Shenzhen, China, in May 2014, by C&C Joint Printing Co., (Guangdong) Ltd. Job #HO0174

A   B   C   D   E   F

 Publisher of Chirp, chickaDEE and OWL
www.owlkidsbooks.com